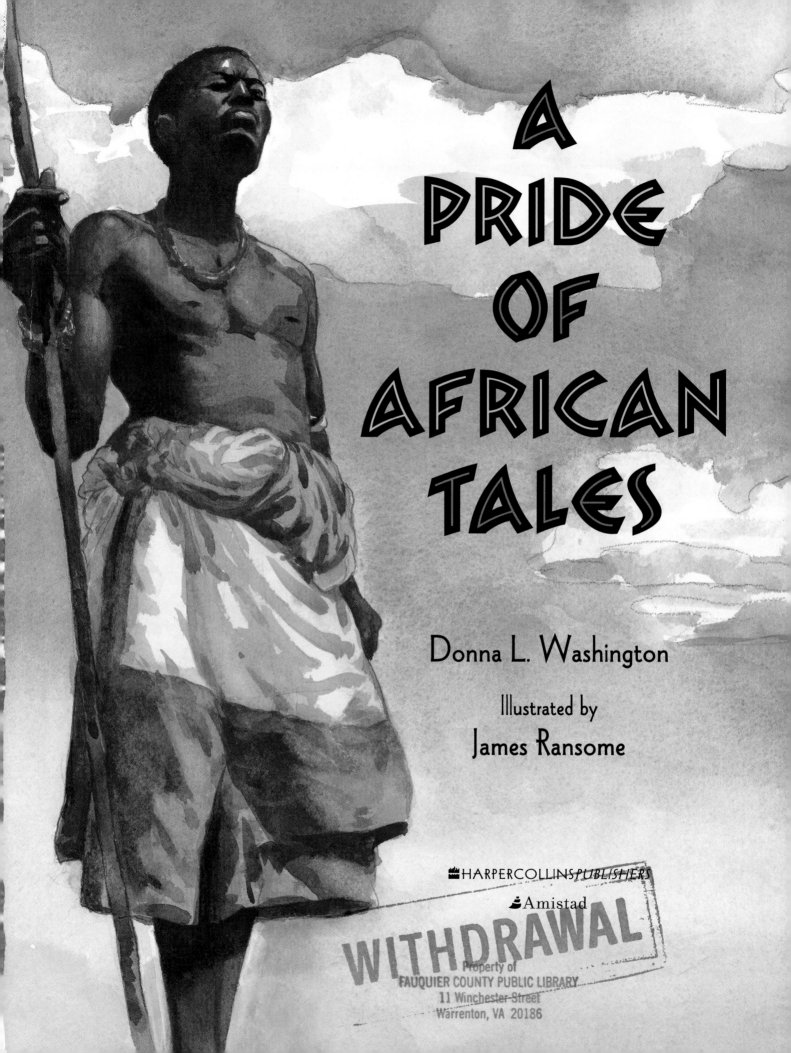

A PRIDE OF AFRICAN TALES

Donna L. Washington

Illustrated by

James Ransome

HARPERCOLLINSPUBLISHERS

Amistad

This book is dedicated to my father. He told
me so many stories when I was a child that I
thought he was thousands of years old. How
else could he have learned so much?
                    —D.L.W.

To Africa
        —J.R.

A PRIDE OF AFRICAN TALES
Text copyright © 2004 by Donna L. Washington
Illustrations copyright © 2004 by James Ransome
Manufactured in China by South China Printing Company Ltd. All rights reserved.
www.harperchildrens.com

Library of Congress Cataloging-in-Publication Data
Washington, Donna.
  A pride of African tales / by Donna L. Washington ; illustrated by James Ransome.
     p.   cm.
  Includes bibliographical references.
  Summary: A collection of African folktales originating in the storytelling
tradition.
  ISBN 0-06-024929-3. — ISBN 0-06-024932-3 (lib. bdg.)
  [1. Folklore—Africa]   I. Ransome, James, ill.   II. Title.
PZ8.1.W28Af   2004
398.2'096—dc20   94-18697
                                                         CIP
                                                         AC

Typography by Elynn Cohen   1 2 3 4 5 6 7 8 9 10 ❖ First Edition

CONTENTS

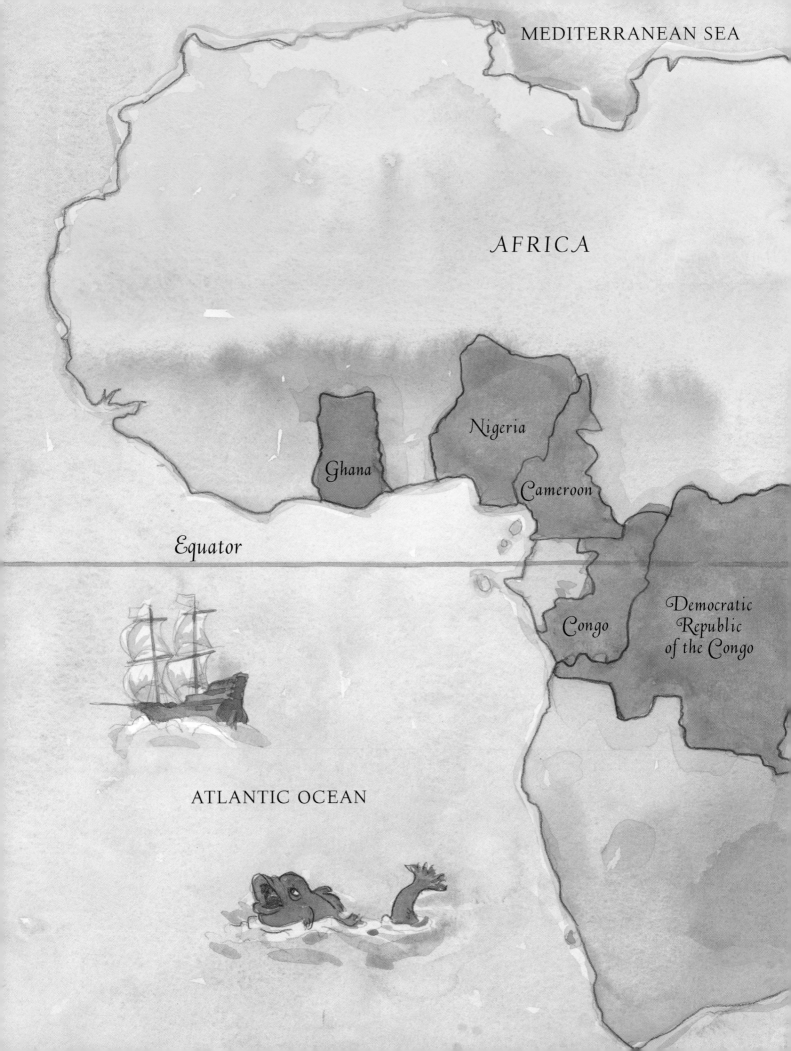

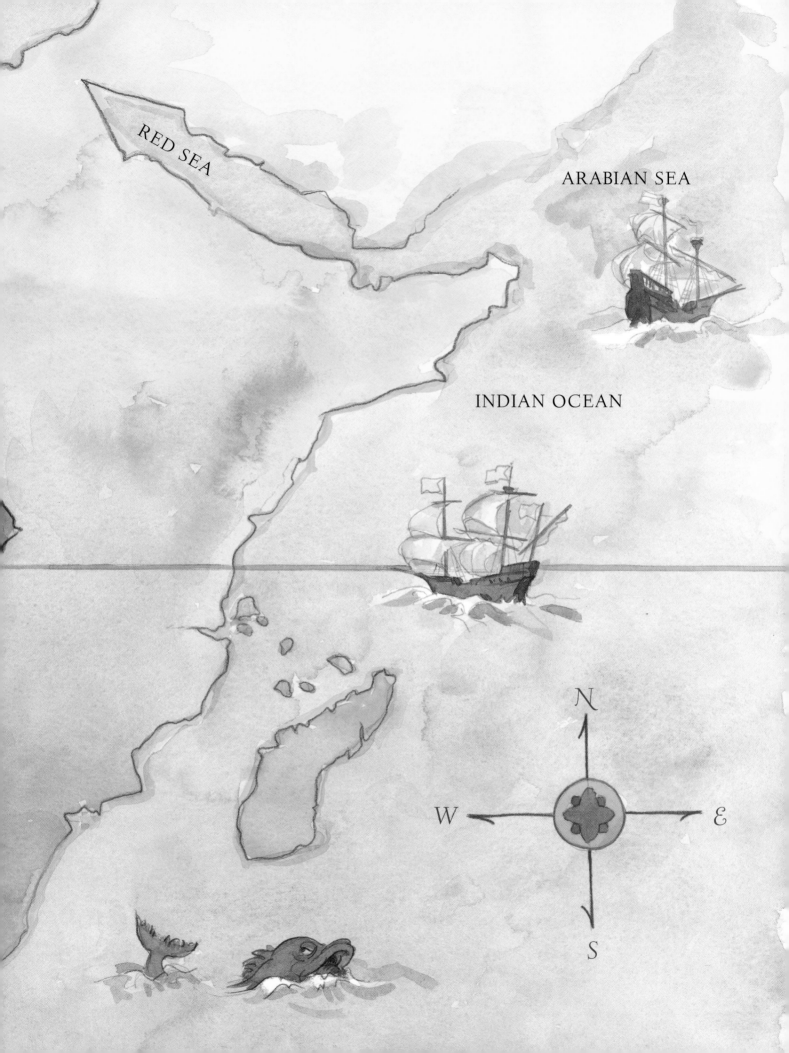

INTRODUCTION

There is something exciting about the power of stories. One minute you are sitting in a very comfortable chair in the living room, and the next you are walking down a road in Africa. Stories can be told to entertain, instruct, remind, or just help communicate. They are the oldest form of art and the best way to pass the time.

When I began putting this collection together, I thought it would be easy. I tell stories all the time. All I had to do was sit down with a pen and some paper and write down the stories the way I tell them. It took no time at all to realize that I was mistaken.

Stories are meant to be *told*. Storytellers create worlds with a movement of the head or a change in tone. They imitate a character's body position as well as take on that character's facial expressions and voice. As a teller tells a story over and over, the story is transformed. It grows and changes until it becomes as individual and personal to the teller as a set of fingerprints. Trying to translate all that onto paper was very difficult!

The stories a person tells can reveal a great deal about the teller. My favorite stories are about people who get exactly what they deserve. I am also fond of tales in which people learn from past mistakes. In this collection each story has two short notes. The first one is at the beginning of the story. It explains a little bit about what kind of story it is. The second note is at the end of the book. It tells where I found the story.

Stories are meant to be told. Please accept my invitation to tell these stories. That is why they exist! Read them, learn them, change them, and, most important of all, enjoy them!

ONE

ANANSI'S FISHING EXPEDITION

A Trickster Tale from Ghana

vvvvvvvvvvvvvvvvvvvvvvvvvvv

Anansi is a trickster. He's always trying to get something for nothing. In this story, though, the tables are turned—it is Anansi who gets tricked!

One day Anansi was sitting beside the road. He got it into his head that he wanted to go fishing. He sat in the sun thinking that it was a good season to catch fish, and if he was successful, he could sell the extra ones in the marketplace. The longer he thought, the surer he was that it was a good idea. He began to think of all the wonderful things he could buy with the money he was going to make, not to mention the fact that he loved to eat fish.

Anansi's daydream was going along just fine until he realized that if he really wanted to have all those fish, he was going to have to do

1

a lot of work. He would have to build traps and then set them and check them every day. The more he thought about the work, the less excited he became. He was just beginning to think that he would have to give the whole thing up when he got an idea.

"I know," he said aloud. "What I need is a partner!"

Anansi hurried to the nearest village. He asked everyone he met to go into business with him, but they all said, "Oh, no, Anansi! I know all about you! Going into business with you means that I will do all the work and you will find some way to cheat me out of all the rewards!"

Anansi tried to look hurt when people said things like this to him, but he had to admit that it was just the sort of thing he had in mind. Finally he got so frustrated that he blurted out, "What I really need is a fool to be my partner!"

When people heard this, they laughed and agreed with him. "You are right, Anansi! Only a great fool would agree to be your partner!"

Well, it just so happened that Onini was in the marketplace that day, and he had heard that Anansi was looking for a fool to be his partner.

Anansi saw Onini around lunchtime and walked over to him. "Onini, I have been looking all over for you! I have a wonderful idea for a business. I want to give you a chance to take advantage of it before I offer it to anyone else." Now, Anansi thought that Onini was a simpleton because he never played practical jokes on anyone and he did not talk much.

"What is it you want, Anansi?" Onini asked, being careful to sound as if he had no idea what Anansi wanted.

"I would like us to go into a partnership together," Anansi said.

"A partnership? Doing what?" Onini asked.

"Fishing!" Anansi responded.

"I think that would be a very good idea, Anansi," Onini said politely.

Anansi smiled to himself. At last he had a fool to go fishing with him.

Everyone tried to warn Onini that Anansi was going to cheat him, but Onini just smiled quietly and said nothing.

Very early the next morning Anansi and Onini went into the forest. Anansi was already forming a plan in his head about how he could make Onini do all the work.

As soon as they got to a place where there were some nice reeds just perfect for fish traps, Onini took out his knife and said to Anansi, "Now, because we are partners, I suggest that we share all the work." Anansi had no intention of sharing the work, but he nodded anyway. "The first thing to do," said Onini, "is to cut the reeds for the traps. I shall cut the reeds."

"What shall I do?" asked Anansi.

"Why, you shall get tired for me, of course. If I have to cut the reeds, I see no reason why you cannot get tired."

"What!" yelped Anansi. "I do not think that is a good idea at all. Why don't you let me cut the reeds, and you can get tired!"

"As you wish, Anansi," said Onini, and he sat in the shade.

For the next hour Anansi cut reeds in the morning sun while Onini panted and stretched his arms as if to ease the muscles. When they had enough reeds to make their traps, Onini said to Anansi, "I sure am tired from all that work. Now I shall carry the reeds to the water, and you may have a sore back for me."

"No you don't!" Anansi cried. "I shall carry the reeds, and you shall get the sore back." Anansi carried the reeds down to the water. Onini made struggling sounds and complained about the great pain in his shoulders. When they got to the water, Onini collapsed in a heap and panted for several minutes as if he had been carrying a mountain on his back.

"Now what?" Anansi asked, knowing that Onini would try to take the easy job.

"Well," said Onini, "we must weave the reeds into fish traps. I shall weave the traps, and you shall have the sore neck and stiff fingers for me."

"Nonsense!" Anansi snapped. "I shall weave the traps, and you may have a sore neck and stiff fingers for me." Onini agreed reluctantly. Anansi sat weaving the fish traps. Onini made a great show of being uncomfortable. Anansi smirked at Onini's discomfort. "What a good idea this was," Anansi said to himself. "Onini is such a fool. Look how much he is suffering."

When the traps were all done, Onini began collecting them. "Wait!" Anansi cried. "What are you doing?"

"Well," Onini answered, "someone has to take the traps out into the deep water.

6

We are partners, after all. So I shall take the traps into the water."

"What am I supposed to do?" Anansi was suspicious.

"There are sharks out there," Onini replied. "If I get bitten, then as my partner you shall die for me."

"WAHH!" Anansi screamed. "Give me those traps! I'll take them out into the deep water, and if a shark bites me, then you shall die!"

And so it was that Anansi waded into the deep water and set the traps.

The two of them agreed to meet the next morning to check them. Onini limped home holding his back and neck. Every now and then he would rest against the trees. Anansi felt kind of sorry for him. Then he smiled and said, "Better him than me."

The next morning the two of them met, and once again Anansi went out to the traps so that he would not have to die if Onini got bitten. There were two huge fish in the traps. Anansi wanted to divide them and give Onini the smaller one, but Onini said, "Oh, no, I don't want either of those little things. I am sure there will be more than just two tomorrow, and they will be twice as big. You can have both of those little things, and I will take all of the catch tomorrow."

Now, in truth, the fish were far from little. They were, in fact, quite large. But as Anansi looked at them, they seemed to shrink.

"I have an idea," Anansi said. "Why don't you take these two, and I will go without today. I will take what we get tomorrow." Onini protested, but Anansi insisted. Finally, Onini took the fish.

The next morning Anansi waded out to the traps, and this time there were four huge fish. Anansi presented them to Onini and laughed at his partner. "What a fool you were to take those two puny fish yesterday! Look at the size and number I have today!"

"Yes," Onini said with a smile, "I see. It makes me very excited, because that means I get all of the catch tomorrow, and I'm sure it will be glorious."

Anansi looked at his four fish. They were big, but they were not glorious.

"Onini," Anansi purred, "why don't you take these fish, and I will take the catch tomorrow." Onini tried to argue, but Anansi was firm.

The next morning Anansi waded out and brought in the traps for the last time. They were rotting by now and would not hold up for

9

even one more night. Inside the traps the catch was glorious. Anansi was very excited. He looked at it and gloated to Onini. "Look, friend, if you had waited even one more day, then all of this would be yours!" But Onini was not even looking at Anansi or his fish. He was looking at the rotted fish traps.

"Please, Anansi," Onini said with excitement, "move your little fish. I want to get these traps to market while they are still in excellent condition."

Anansi looked at the fish traps. They were many things. They were rotten, they were falling apart, they were a little smelly, and they were slimy. What they were not was in excellent condition. Anansi became suspicious.

"What do you mean, 'in excellent condition'?" he asked as he slowly emptied all of his "little" fish out of the traps.

"These will fetch a handsome price at market!" Onini said as he gathered together the rotted, stinking fish traps.

"Wait a minute!" Anansi gritted his teeth. "I made those fish traps."

"I know," Onini said impatiently, "but if you are going to keep the fish, you may as well let me take the traps."

"No! I'll keep the traps and you keep the little fish."

Anansi gathered up the fish traps and went on his way. Onini smiled to himself as he collected the mass of huge fish. He walked to the village and thought about how well he had done in the market that week.

Onini was moving at a considerably slower pace than Anansi, so he missed all the fun back in the village. When he arrived at the marketplace, everyone was laughing hysterically.

"What's so funny?" Onini asked.

"Anansi, your partner," a woman said, choking with laughter, "came to market with these rotted fish traps to sell. He stank up the market so badly that the chief was called. He got a beating for disrupting the market, and now he's asking for you."

Onini was amused. "What does he want with me? By now I hope he realizes that the only fool he went fishing with was himself."

"Well," said the woman, laughing again, "he had just finished getting his beating when he shouted: 'Where is that lousy partner of mine, Onini! If I had to take this beating, the least he could have done was to take the pain!'"

T W O

THE BOY WHO WANTED THE MOON

A Pourquoi Tale from the Congo

wwwwwwwwwwwwwwwwww

Pourquoi tales are told to explain why the world is the way it is.
They tell us why birds fly, why the crow is black, or why, as in this story,
there are monkeys in the world. It is a story about a spoiled child,
his doting father, and a great deal of foolishness.

There was once a great king in west Africa. He had many wives and
many daughters but only one son. The king loved his son so much
that he gave the boy everything. At the age of six the prince had his
own house. He had exquisite clothes, and his arms and ears jingled
with gold and silver. The prince was carried around in a chair. He
didn't walk unless he felt like it.

The king made his son the king of all the children in his kingdom.
Because there were more children than adults in the kingdom, the

son had more subjects than the father. Unfortunately, all the things his father gave him did not satisfy the prince. The more he had, the more he wanted.

Every day the little prince would hold council in the marketplace. He would make all the children of the village sit very still before him and watch him eat his lunch.

Then they would have to sit very still and watch him get his face washed.

Then they would have to watch the little prince take a nap in the sun.

The children were not allowed to leave until they were dismissed. None of the children liked the prince.

One day the prince announced, "I am the greatest child who ever lived! And I have everything."

A little girl sitting in the marketplace had had enough of the prince. She stood up and said, "No, you don't! You don't have everything!"

"Yes, I do!" the haughty prince replied. "Tell me something I do not have."

"You don't have the moon." She sneered. When they heard this, the other children burst out laughing.

At first the prince was outraged. Then he realized the little girl was right. He did not have the moon. He dismissed his subjects and stomped off to find his father. He marched right up to him and said, "Father, I want the moon."

His father just looked at him. "You are joking."

"No." The prince was annoyed. "I am not joking. I want the moon."

The king shook his head. "I cannot give you the moon."

No one had ever said no to the prince. The little boy was shocked. Then he closed his eyes, clenched his fists, and began to wail. Large tears ran down his brown cheeks.

"If you don't give me the moon," he screamed at the top of his lungs, "I will sit in my house for the rest of my life! I will refuse to talk or eat! I will be miserable for the rest of my days!" He ran to his house.

The king was worried. He did not want his son to be miserable. He called the wise people of the village together and said, "You must find a way to get the moon for my son."

The wise people stared at one another. "Sir," one of them asked with respect, "are you making a joke?"

"No." The king was rather annoyed. "I am not joking! Get the moon for my son! He is miserable without it."

One of the wise people leaned forward. "Consider, sir. Your son is a young, healthy boy. Surely he will get over this in time. Besides, what you ask is rather serious. The gods put the moon in the sky for a reason. I think it would be wise to leave it up there."

The king folded his arms. "My son is the most important thing upon this earth! If he wants the moon, he must have it!"

The king would not be swayed. So the wise ones began planning how to get the moon. After much debate they came up with an idea.

"Sir, if you want the moon, this is what you must do. All the warriors in your kingdom must work together for the next ten years building a scaffolding to the sky. At the end of those ten years you must climb to the top of that scaffolding. During

the deepest part of the night the moon will pass right over your head. All you have to do is reach up and pull it out of the sky."

The king was very pleased with his wise people. He walked away, ignoring the warnings they shouted after him.

For the next ten years everyone in the kingdom devoted their energy to building a scaffolding to the sky. The wise people kept hoping that the prince would lose interest in the moon as he grew older or that the king would come to his senses. Neither of those things happened.

At the end of the ten years the king, the prince, and all the people from the kingdom climbed onto the scaffolding. At the deepest part of the night the moon passed right over their heads, and the king reached up his hands. Everyone held their breath as he touched the moon.

"AACH!" The king yelped, and drew back his hands. He blew on his palms to cool them. The king turned to his son. "You cannot have the moon. It is too hot."

The prince was now a young man of sixteen. He was strong, spoiled, and stubborn. If you cannot tell someone what to do when he is six, you have no hope when he turns sixteen. "I have been waiting for the moon for ten years!" he hissed. "I will have it!" The prince reached up and grabbed the moon. Smoke curled from his hands as he pulled with all his might.

Without warning, the moon broke. Pieces of hot moon rock showered down on the people. The scaffolding burst into flame.

The king, his son, and all of their subjects began falling to the earth.

Everyone surely would have died if it had not been for the gods. The gods of Africa took pity on all those foolish people and caught them in their hands. They let them live, but to punish them for trying to undo what the gods themselves had done, they turned all the people into monkeys.

You can see their descendants all over the world swinging through the trees. They are there as a warning to other foolish people.

THREE

SHANSA MUTONGO SHIMA

A Cautionary Tale from the Democratic Republic of the Congo

*Cautionary tales are told to impart warnings and give advice.
"Shansa Mutongo Shima" carries a warning about strangers
and the dangers of judging people by appearances alone.*

People, I will tell you of a little thing, a little, little thing. There was a girl and her name was Bwalya. And, people, she was very, very clever. Bwalya had a quick mind and she could make people laugh. Not only that, people, but she was also very beautiful. Because she was so clever and beautiful, you know that all the men in her village wanted to marry her. They brought many things for her bride price.

"Look, Bwalya, I bring you these shells from the deep sea," said one. Another pushed forward. "I bring you yams from the brown earth, beautiful Bwalya." And still another spoke up. "I have a fine house for you, dear Bwalya."

Now, people, even though these men were kind and worthy, none of them were as clever as Bwalya. You can see how it was. She did not find any of them very interesting. And so, people, Bwalya turned all of them away with a smile. She did not want to marry any of them.

Then one day from far away there came a stranger. He was very, very handsome and extremely charming. He wore a high top hat and a three-piece suit, and he had a pocket watch. And, people, he was very, very clever.

This man made everyone laugh with his stories. This man had traveled to many places in Africa, and he had met many interesting people and done many interesting things. When Bwalya met him, people, you know she fell in love with him. The other people of her village thought he was interesting, but they did not trust him.

"Bwalya!" one woman said to her. "What could you possibly want with this stranger? Are there not enough handsome men from our village to please you?"

"There are more than enough handsome men from this village," said Bwalya, "but there are not any clever ones!" The two of them laughed about that, but it did not make the woman feel any better.

Well, people, there came a day when this stranger asked Bwalya to marry him. And you know she said yes. Bwalya's father announced to the village that Bwalya would marry this stranger, this

man whose name was Shansa
Mutongo Shima.

Well, people, at first the villagers did
not approve. Bwalya's father told them
that there would be ten days of
feasting before the wedding. He
hoped that all the festivities
would help the people look
on Shansa Mutongo Shima
with more kindness.

On the first day of
the festival, people,
Shansa Mutongo Shima
brought a gift to the
village. He brought many
game animals for the feast. Everyone was
very pleased.

Every morning after that Shansa
Mutongo Shima went out into the bush,
and every day he returned to the village with
his arms laden with
game animals.
Nobody knew how
he did it. Sometimes
hunters would go

out into the bush for a long time, and they would not catch anything. But every day Shansa Mutongo Shima returned with his arms laden with game animals. The villagers did not know how he could do this, people, and they did not care. They were happy to have a hunter who could bring back so much meat. They did not care, people, but they should have cared. You see, Shansa Mutongo Shima was a shape changer.

Every day he would go out into the bush and take off his human skin, and underneath it was a lion. Then he would dance and sing.

"I am Shansa Mutongo Shima!
I come to see Bwalya.
Beware! Shansa Mutongo Shima comes here today!"

People, when Shansa Mutongo Shima did this, I will tell you what happened. The animals would come out of the bush and dance. They would dance and dance without stopping. They would dance until they fell down dead. Then Shansa Mutongo Shima would take their bodies back to the village.

The people of Bwalya's village now called this man friend. Everyone was content that the wedding should take place. Everyone, people, except Bwalya. She was growing very suspicious about this man she was supposed to marry.

"How can you hunt so well?" she asked Shansa Mutongo Shima.

"Ah," he said. "No hunter is as clever as I. I can catch anything."

"But how do you do it?" she asked again. The stranger did not answer. He only smiled.

The next day, people, Bwalya waited for Shansa Mutongo Shima to go hunting. Then she went hiding. Bwalya went hiding. She saw Shansa Mutongo Shima take off his human skin to reveal the lion underneath. Then he began to dance and sing.

> *"I am Shansa Mutongo Shima!*
> *I come to see Bwalya.*
> *The one who thinks she is so clever.*
> *Beware! Shansa Mutongo Shima comes here today!"*

Bwalya ran back to the village. She knew that no one would believe her if she told them what she had seen. The villagers knew that she had second thoughts about getting married. They would say that she had made this story up to get out of the wedding. You see, people, the villagers had been charmed by Shansa Mutongo Shima. So Bwalya decided to take matters into her own hands.

First she went to her father and said, "Father, tomorrow we shall go for a walk. There are things I would talk to you about before I am married and gone." Well, people, her father agreed to walk with her.

The next day the two of them walked together and talked of many things. Bwalya's father did not know it, but Bwalya was leading him to the place where Shansa Mutongo Shima did his hunting. Well, you know what they saw when they got there. Shansa Mutongo Shima was just taking off his human skin to let the lion

31

out into the sunshine. When he was finished, he began to dance and sing.

> "I am Shansa Mutongo Shima!
> I come to see Bwalya.
> The one who thinks she is so clever!
> I am Shansa Mutongo Shima!
> I can charm animals.
> Beware! Shansa Mutongo Shima comes here today!"

They ran back to the village. Bwalya's father went straight to Bwalya's uncle and told him about the stranger. Now, people, Bwalya's uncle, like the rest of the people in the village, liked having a lot of fresh meat. When Bwalya's father told him about Shansa Mutongo Shima, he got very angry.

"Bwalya," said Bwalya's uncle, "this is foolishness! You have decided not to marry him because he is more clever than you are! And you," he said to Bwalya's father, "you are just jealous because he wears such fine clothes and is a better hunter than you are! He is not a lion! I will go with you tomorrow and I will prove it!"

And so, people, the next day they went hiding. They went hiding. And they watched Shansa Mutongo Shima take off his human skin, and underneath it was a lion. Then he began to dance and sing.

> "I am Shansa Mutongo Shima!
> I come to see Bwalya.
> The one who thinks she is so clever!
> I am Shansa Mutongo Shima!
> I can charm animals. I kill animals!
> Beware! Shansa Mutongo Shima comes here today!"

The three of them ran back to the village. At first, people, you know the men wanted to tell the elders, but Bwalya stopped them.

"I have a better plan," she told them.

"Well," said her father, "it had better be a good one, because tomorrow is the wedding! I am not going to let you marry a lion!"

"Trust me," Bwalya said to her father.

"I will show this Shansa Mutongo Shima that I am as clever as I think I am!" she said to herself.

That night Bwalya, her father, and her uncle crept to the place where Shansa Mutongo Shima was sleeping. People, I will tell you what they took with them. They took four leopard skins, six bamboo sticks, and a pair of antlers.

The three of them stood in the shadows and draped three of the leopard skins over their bodies. Then, people, Bwalya put the antlers on top of her head and climbed onto her father's back. Bwalya's uncle put the last leopard skin over Bwalya and her father to make them look like one creature, and then he bent over behind them. When Bwalya raised her arms, all three of them began to wave their bamboo sticks in the air and beat them together.

Now, people, when Shansa Mutongo Shima heard all this noise, you know he sprang up from his sleeping place and looked out through his door. He saw a gigantic shape outside. It was furry, with a huge hump on its back, horns, four legs, and six long, thin arms. It was crashing its long arms together and swaying. Then it began to move slowly toward his house singing a song. At first Shansa Mutongo Shima could not make out what the creature was saying. Then, bit by bit, he heard it. This is the song it was singing.

"I am Bwalya the Hungry One!
I search for Shansa Mutongo Shima.
The one who is a lion!
I am Bwalya the Hungry One! I will eat anything.
Tonight I will eat a lion!
Beware! Bwalya the Hungry One comes here tonight!"

Well, people, when Shansa Mutongo Shima heard that great monster, he tore off his human skin and ran out of the village as fast as he could.

The next day Bwalya went to the wedding place and waited. Shansa Mutongo Shima did not come. Everyone was shocked and angry. They turned to Bwalya and said many things about how foolish she had been to choose a stranger with no honor.

"This is what comes of trusting strangers! See how he has broken his word and brought dishonor to our village! Well, clever Bwalya, we hope you have learned a lesson!"

Two years later, people, Bwalya married a man. This man was also a stranger. At first everyone was very angry. However, this man turned out to be a good husband and father. It is said, people, that Bwalya grew old surrounded by her children and grandchildren. Many times she would tell them what I have been trying to tell you with this little story.

"What lies inside a person is much more important than what you see on the outside. You must take your time, watch, and listen before you make your final decision about a person."

And that, people, is all.

THE ROOF OF LEAVES

A Tale of Anger and Forgiveness from the Congo

wwwwwwwwwwwwwww

This story is based on a real incident. It is about a man and a woman and the quick thinking that saves them both from making a big mistake.

Once a man and a woman who had loved each other for a long time came together as man and wife. The people of the village, to celebrate the marriage, built them a beautiful house. It had a roof of bright-green leaves. The two of them were very happy.

But one morning they were in a bad mood. They started arguing. Then they started yelling. The two of them became so angry, they forgot many things. They forgot that they had spent a great deal of time together laughing and talking in the shadows of the great

39

trees. They forgot that they were in love. They forgot that they were happy. The husband got so angry that he ran out of their house.

Once outside, the husband, in his fury, laid his hands on the first thing he saw and began to rip it apart. This thing was the roof of his house.

He was so angry that he did not even realize what he was doing. He had forgotten that when either the husband or the wife pulls all the leaves off the roof of their house, it means "I divorce you; we will no longer live beneath the same roof."

The wife came outside. As she watched her husband pull leaves off their house, she saw how full of anger he was. It made her remember that he could also be full of joy. He loved to laugh, and he could sing better than anyone else in the village. He was also one of the best storytellers.

The wife was going to say something when she noticed people coming out of their houses. "If I say something," she thought, "they'll think I'm to blame for this argument. I won't say anything unless my husband speaks first."

The husband began to pull the leaves slower and slower. He realized what he was doing. He didn't want to divorce his wife. Now that his anger was leaving him, he couldn't even remember why they had argued.

Just as he was about to stop pulling the leaves, he saw his wife and all the villagers watching him. "If I stop pulling the leaves, everyone will think this argument was my fault. Well, I won't stop until my wife says something."

The people of the village looked from the husband to the wife. They were astonished. They knew the two of them loved each other. All the neighbors wanted to say something, but it was not a good idea to come between a man and his wife.

It seemed there was no hope for the situation.

Everyone was silent. The wife watched the husband, the husband pulled leaves off the roof, and the neighbors looked around sadly.

"Husband," the wife said, so suddenly that everyone jumped, "these are the only leaves that are dirty. You can leave the rest of them up there."

The husband looked at his wife with confusion. "I said," she repeated slowly, "these are the only leaves that are dirty. Come, let us take them down to the river."

Without waiting to see if he was doing what she said, she began to gather up the fallen leaves. The husband stood there for a moment, confused, and then he began to smile and collect the leaves with his wife.

They took them down to the river and washed them in the water. Then they laid them out to dry in the sun and went swimming. Afterward, they collected the leaves and replaced them on the roof together.

On that day every wife went to her husband and mentioned something about the dirty leaves on top of their own homes. Together, husbands and wives removed leaves from the roofs of their houses, washed them in the river, and dried them in the sun. That had never happened before in the village. As far as we know, it never happened again. The best that can be hoped for is that we remember that we can always wash the leaves.

FIVE

THE WEDDING BASKET

A Taboo Story from Nigeria

〰〰〰〰〰〰〰〰〰〰〰

A taboo is something that is forbidden. The breaking
of a taboo is serious business and can have disastrous
results—as the hero of this tale discovers.

Once there was a very rich man. He had many beautiful things and servants to attend to his every wish. He was a very fortunate man.

The only thing the rich man did not have was a wife. He looked long and hard, but he had never found anyone he thought worthy. He had many things to offer a wife. He knew he'd make a fine husband. After all, he was a very fortunate man.

The rich man's most prized possessions were his white cows. In his village white cows were a rarity. A man who owned one was looked upon as a fortunate man. The rich man owned not one but seven.

45

Every morning after milking his cows, the rich man would take them to pasture. All the people would stare at the beautiful animals. He could almost hear them whispering among themselves. "Of course he is a rich man. Look at how the gods favor him."

One morning the man went out to milk his cows.

"Good morning to you, ladies," he greeted them. He took down a pail, placed it beneath the nearest cow, and sat down to milk her. To his surprise, the cow was dry. The rich man was astonished. In all his years, none of his cows had ever gone dry. "What is the matter,

lady? Didn't you get enough to eat yesterday?" He went to the next cow. She too was dry. The same was true of all of his cows.

The rich man went into his house and began to pace. "All these years my cows have given me milk, and now all of them have gone dry! Perhaps the field I was grazing them in was not sweet enough. Today I will take them to a different field."

The rich man led his cows to a fertile green valley that he normally reserved for times of drought. He let the cows stay to graze a little longer than usual before he led them home.

In the morning, however, his cows were as dry as they had been the day before. "Hmmm," the man mused to himself, "perhaps they need an even sweeter pasture."

The rich man led his cows far from the village that day. They went deep into the mountains to a valley that was shielded on all sides from weather. The grass here was lush and green. Running through the middle of the valley was a little stream. He let his cows graze until very late before he took them home.

In the morning, however, his cows were as dry as they had been for the last two days. "This makes no sense!" he fumed aloud. "I have let them eat the sweetest grass in Africa and still they do not make milk. There has to be another solution." As these words passed his lips, he got an idea. "Perhaps someone is sneaking into my stables and stealing my milk. Tonight I will stay awake and I will keep watch."

That night the rich man hid in his stables and watched. He nodded off a great deal, but he was certain that no one had been near his cows. He was just about to give up and go in to sleep when something strange happened.

Out of the sky fell seven golden threads. They shimmered and danced like moonbeams. Descending on these threads were seven beautiful maidens. Each of them carried on her head a bowl that glistened like silver. The maidens came to rest on the ground in front of the cows. Each maiden went to a cow and began milking her.

The rich man was amazed. He could not draw his eyes away from the beautiful women. In fact, it wasn't until they were leaving that he remembered why he was there at all.

"Stop!" he cried, jumping out from his place of concealment. The women saw him and began running for their golden threads. The rich man bounded toward the women and managed to catch one of them. The others scurried up their golden threads. The rich man looked at the beautiful woman in his arms and his heart caught in his throat. Her skin was dark and smooth, and her eyes were a soft hazel. He forgot all about his cows. Here at last was a woman who was worthy to be his wife.

"I am sorry I startled you." The rich man smiled. "But you are stealing my milk. This is a very serious thing. I will forgive this theft only if you promise to marry me."

The beautiful maiden smiled right back. "I am the daughter of Nyami, the sky god. My sisters and I meant no harm. We don't get much milk in our father's kingdom."

The maiden kept trying to go home, but the rich man held her tight. He promised that her sisters could have all the milk they wanted if she would agree to marry him.

The rich man kept telling Nyami's daughter that he would make a wonderful husband. He charmed her with his words and his smile. Eventually, she agreed to marry him. "There is only one thing I ask," she said as she prepared to climb up the golden thread to speak to her father about the marriage. "When I come to your house, I shall have a basket. You are not to look into it until I say it is all right."

The rich man was so happy, he would have agreed to anything. He was relieved she hadn't asked for anything difficult.

The wedding took place. Now the rich man had the biggest house in the village, seven white cows, many servants, and the most beautiful wife anyone had ever seen. No one was as fortunate as he was.

Three months after the marriage, the rich man was home alone. He looked up and saw on a shelf his wife's wedding basket. For the first time he remembered his promise. He wondered what was so private that his wife could not share it with him.

Well, it certainly did not matter to him what she had in her silly old basket. However, there was something right next to the basket that he needed. He reached up and pushed the basket by accident. It moved very easily. The rich man frowned. Then he knocked it off the shelf by accident. The lid did not come off when it hit the floor.

The rich man stared at the aggravating basket for a few minutes, and then he got angry. "I am the man of this house," he said under his breath. "What right has my wife to keep anything from me? I am her husband, her guardian, her provider, and she owes me the respect of not keeping secrets from me. It is my right to look into this basket, because everything she owns I own, and who in all this world can tell me that I cannot look into my own basket!"

The rich man pounced on the basket and removed the lid. He took one look inside, made a perplexed face, and then began to laugh. He laughed and laughed and laughed. He put the lid back on, replaced the basket on the shelf, and sat on the floor laughing.

That is how his wife found him an hour later, sitting on the floor laughing.

As soon as she saw him, she knew what had happened. "Did you look in my basket?" she asked.

The rich man sat there with tears running out of his eyes because he had been laughing so much and said, "Yes, dear, I did. I'm afraid I was unable to resist. I looked in your basket." At this, he began laughing again.

His wife pursed her lips. Her husband was laughing so hard that he did not even notice. He didn't see the offended expression cross her face. "I see. Well, I'm going home to my father."

The rich man stopped laughing.

"What do you mean, you are going home to your father? I'm sorry I looked in your basket, I really am. But honestly, I don't understand what you are so upset about. There was nothing in it!"

His wife looked at him for a second, and then she said in a quiet voice, "You are wrong. There are many things in my basket. Things that are important to me that I had hoped to show you someday. I am not leaving because you could not see any of those special things all by yourself. I'm leaving because you laughed!"

The rich man begged Nyami's daughter to stay with him. She turned away from him and would not listen. That night he watched as she climbed out of sight.

Many things about the rich man changed after Nyami's daughter left. He no longer escorted his cows out to pasture. He spent more time with his neighbors. He often had a word of encouragement for others.

The years passed, and the rich man married another woman. The two of them were very happy. They had many children, and the rich man's life was filled with joy and laughter.

In the evenings he would sit with his children.

"You must respect people's dreams," he would say. "You see, my children, anyone who cannot respect others is not worthy of respect himself."

The rich man's words were not lost on his children. They passed them down to their children. Now I am passing them on to you.

SIX

THE TALKING SKULL

A Fable from Cameroon

wwwwwwwwwwwwwwwww

"The Talking Skull" is an African fable about the importance
of listening and thinking before opening one's mouth.

Once a man was walking down the road toward his village. He was
not paying attention to anything around him. This man considered
himself a scholar of life. He was always deep in thought. He liked
to think about important things. He did not put his mind to ordi-
nary problems. If it wasn't impossible, or at least very complicated,
he didn't care about it at all.

This man spent all day looking out over the ocean, and he only
noticed things he thought were useful. He didn't notice the beauty
of the ocean. The only things he considered were sharks and ship-
wrecks. He didn't notice the clear blue sky. He was thinking about

59

all the storms that must have been churning far away. He did not notice the wonderful songs of the birds. He only thought about how many of their nests had been robbed. He didn't notice the playful animals swinging through branches or rustling in the grass. He only wondered whether or not the great cats were on the prowl. That was the kind of man he was.

As he walked back toward the village that day, he happened to pass a pile of bones. They were bleached white and they gleamed in the bright sun. He stopped and stared down at them. He was the sort of man who would stop to stare down at a pile of bones. The skull on the pile was resting above all the other bones, and it seemed to be watching the man just as intently as he was watching it.

The man reached out and picked up the skull. He held it one way and then another. He looked gravely into the empty eye sockets and said, "What brought you here, brother?"

"Talking," the skull replied without much interest.

The man was so shocked, he dropped the skull and jumped back. He watched the skull for a few minutes before he managed to stammer out, "You can talk!"

"Yes," said the skull. "Talking is very easy. All you have to do is open up your mouth and out it comes. Talking is easy. Finding something worthwhile to say is not."

The man was amazed. He had never seen a talking skull before, let alone one that could spout such wisdom. "I must take you to the village!" the man exclaimed.

He scooped up the skull and ran as fast as he could. The villagers saw him coming, and a great many of them ran for their homes.

You see, he was the kind of man who was always getting busy people into useless conversations when there was work to be done. He never seemed to be quiet, and he never spoke about anything anyone ever wanted to hear.

As he entered the village, he called out to his neighbors, "Come quickly! I have something wonderful to show you!" No one came.

The man was so excited that he did not even realize that the few people in sight were moving away from him. "Put down whatever you are doing, everyone! I have a marvelous mystery to show all of you, the likes of which you have never before seen!"

When the man said the word "mystery," you can be sure he got the attention of some of the villagers. They started poking their heads out of their houses. Women left their yams cooking, men put down their digging sticks, and children stopped their playing. They all began to gather around the man.

When he saw that he had everyone's attention, he drew out the skull. He could not have prepared himself for what happened next.

Everyone stared at the skull for a moment. Then they all started yelling.

"Mama! What is he doing?" cried a little boy.

"How dare you bring that thing here!" his mother howled, waving a spoon.

"Somebody do something!" said another, clutching her child.

"Send him away!" demanded a third mother.

The men who still had gardening tools in their hands started waving them.

"Move out of the way!" yelled a man with a digging stick.

"Somebody get the chief!" said an old man holding his grandson's hand.

There was so much commotion, the chief came to see what was happening.

"What is going on?" the chief roared. He was a very orderly chief, and he did not like all this yelling and brandishing of gardening tools in the middle of the village.

All the people were silent except for one villager. He stood up and pointed to the man with the skull.

"This man told us he had something to show us. Then he pulled out

that awful skull. We thought he was trying to call the Dark Spirits to the village, and we were trying to stop him."

"Oh," said the chief, eyeing the man with the skull. "And were you going to call Dark Spirits to my village?"

"Certainly not!" the scholar declared, glad that the chief was there. He was sure the chief would understand this intellectual matter.

"Then what were you doing?" the chief asked with curiosity.

"Well," the man said in a pompous voice, "I was on my way home from the ocean when I came across a pile of bones. On top of the heap was this skull. It spoke to me! I brought it here to share this wonder with the village."

The chief did not look convinced.

"I'll show you," the man said, raising the skull so that it looked at the chief. "Say something to the chief," he commanded.

The skull said nothing. The chief frowned.

"Speak!" the man said. "I command you!"

The skull remained silent. One of the children laughed.

"Speak!" he said. "You must speak!" The man started getting nervous.

The skull said nothing. The man begged and pleaded with the skull. The skull remained silent. The people began to get angry again, and the chief got angry right along with them.

"You are always a troublemaker in my village, and now you come here with this nonsense!" The chief and the people had had enough. They took the skull from the man, found the mound of bones he had taken it from, and put it back there.

That very day the villagers held a meeting with the chief and

decided to throw the man out of their village. They watched him collect his few belongings and said to him, "Since you found that skull so much company, why don't you go live with it!"

The man stormed out of the village and down the road to the pile of bones. He picked up the skull. Before he could get one word out of his mouth, the skull said, "Sorry about that."

"What? Now you talk! That is not going to do me much good! Why didn't you say something back in the village?"

"I told you," the skull replied. "It is easy to talk. It is not always easy to find something worthwhile to say."

"You are absolutely unpleasant!" the man screamed. "I don't know what trouble you caused that brought you to this sorry state, but you deserve everything you got!"

"I already told you what got me into trouble," the skull replied. "Talking. Same as you."

STORY NOTES AND
FURTHER READING

∿∿∿∿∿∿∿∿∿∿∿∿∿∿∿∿∿∿

Anansi's Fishing Expedition

The Asante, or Ashanti, nation, where people first told stories about Anansi, is located in southwest Ghana. Stories about Anansi can be found all over Africa as well as in the Caribbean. Anansi is most often depicted as a spider and is sometimes called Grandfather Spider. But in spider or human form, Anansi is always the same—wily, conniving, and full of schemes. More stories about Anansi can be found in the following books:

Appiah, Peggy. *Ananse the Spider: Tales from an Ashanti Village*. Illus. Peggy Wilson. New York: Pantheon, 1966.

Arkhurst, Joyce Cooper. *The Adventures of Spider: West African Folk Tales*. Illus. Jerry Pinkney. Boston: Little, Brown, 1964.

Courlander, Harold, and George Herzog. *The Cow-Tail Switch and Other West African Stories*. Illus. Madye Lee Chastain. New York: Holt, Rinehart, 1947.

The Boy Who Wanted the Moon

This story comes from the Congo. It is one of many stories where foolish people are turned into monkeys. Below are some sources for this one, as well as other related stories.

Aardema, Verna. *Tales from the Story Hat*. Illus. Elton Fax. New York: Coward-McCann, 1960.

Finger, Charles Joseph. *Tales from Silver Lands*. Illus. Paul Honoré. Garden City, NY: Doubleday, 1924.

Leach, Maria. *How the People Sang the Mountains Up: How and Why Stories*. Illus. Glen Rounds. New York: Viking, 1967.

Shansa Mutongo Shima

I first encountered the Tabwa version of this tale during a literature class when I was in college. The Tabwa people live in the area now known as the Democratic Republic of the Congo, formerly Zaire. Since then I have heard many more versions of this tale from all over Africa. It is so popular that a storyteller's audience will often interrupt the telling to point out differences from the version they know or to ask questions. It is then the storyteller's job to improvise a bit and incorporate elements the audience may suggest.

Cancel, Robert. *Allegorical Speculation in an Oral Society: The Tabwa Narrative Tradition.* Berkeley, CA: University of California Press, 1989.

Faustin, Charles. *Under the Storyteller's Spell: Folk Tales from the Caribbean.* Illus. Rossetta Woolf. London: Viking, 1989.

The Roof of Leaves

This is based on an event documented by Colin Turnbull. Colin Turnbull lived and worked with the people of the Ituri forest in the Congo region. I first heard this story from a performer named Rebecca Armstrong.

Turnbull, Colin. *The Forest People.* New York: Simon & Schuster/Touchstone, 1961.

The Wedding Basket

We know that this story comes from somewhere in west Africa, but since it is a story from the oral tradition, its sources are hard to pin down. I have never seen it in print. The illustrator set the story in Nigeria.

The Talking Skull

This story is said to have originated in west Africa, but there are many different versions of it. I have created this one by combining several different variations. In his illustrations the artist used Cameroon for his setting.

Frobenius, Leo, and Douglas C. Fox. *African Genesis.* New York: Benjamin Blom, 1937, 1966.

Leach, Maria. *The Thing at the Foot of the Bed and Other Scary Tales.* Illus. Kurt Werth. Cleveland: World, 1959.

Littledale, Freya. *Ghosts and Spirits of Many Lands.* Illus. Stefan Martin. Garden City, NY: Doubleday, 1970.